OLAF'S SAGA

For Prof Sawyer

who introduced me to the Vikings

P.G.

To Andrew and Noah, my Canadian

grand-nephews (aged six and four)

R.L.

First published in Great Britain 2003
by Egmont Books Ltd
239 Kensington High Street, London W8 6SA
Text copyright © Pippa Goodhart 2003
Illustrations copyright © Robin Lawrie 2003
The author and illustrator have asserted their moral rights
Paperback ISBN 1 4052 0588 1
10 9 8 7 6 5 4 3 2 1
A CIP catalogue record for this title is available from the British Library
Printed in U.A.E.

OLAF'S SAGA

Pippa Goodhart

Robin Lawrie

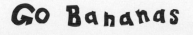

GO Bananas

CHAPTER 1

ONE NIGHT HAL and Grandfather had sat up late together in the soft flickering candlelight.

Long after the homestead was hushed with sleep, Grandfather's dog, Freya, had given a great heave and, one after another, four little puppies had come out of her. Grandfather didn't name the puppies straight away. 'Wait and see if they take strong hold of life before we name them,' he said.

One of the puppies did die that night. But the other three were strong and Freya licked and loved them and let them feed from her.

But by the time the sun rose, Grandfather himself was ill.

The fever came on Grandfather and he lay by the fire under wolf skins the same grizzled grey as his own beard, and he shivered terribly.

Hal's uncle came when he heard. They all prayed to Odin Allfather to save Grandfather. They killed his horse in offering to the gods, but the great god Odin wanted Grandfather for himself and so he died.

They buried Grandfather together with his horse and his great sword and his axe.

They killed Freya too. Hal went away and
covered his ears and scrunched his eyes tight
shut when they did that. But Grandfather
had to have his animals to help him in
the afterlife.

'What about the puppies?' asked Hal.

'They are not needed,' said
big Uncle Ivar. Hal thought
that Uncle Ivar blamed
the puppies for keeping
Grandfather up on a cold
night and making him ill.

Hal saw Uncle Ivar go to the barn and come out again with the three little dogs. There were stones tied with cords around each puppy's neck. Hal watched his uncle stride down to the water's edge and throw the puppies into the sea. But as soon as Uncle Ivar had gone, Hal rushed down to where he had stood. Quick as a fish in the icy cold, Hal darted down, searching the wobbly water and stony sea bed for Freya's puppies. Only one of them was fighting the water, struggling against the weight of the stone that held it down. Hal reached for that puppy, slipped the cord from around its neck and lifted it into the air. Then Hal waded ashore and ran with the puppy clutched close. He must find a safe secret place for them both.

What Hal didn't know was that he was being followed.

CHAPTER 2

CLUTCHING THE LIMP, wet puppy, Hal hurried up past the homestead buildings to the place where the sides of the fjord rose steeply. He climbed, panting, zig zagging up and up, heading for a big rock that seemed frozen in mid-tumble down the slope. The rock was big and grey and wedge-shaped. Hal called it Thor's Hammer after the weapon used by the god of war. He felt safe there.

A sudden scatter of stones behind Hal made him whip around.

'Gudrun!'

Gudrun was Hal's big cousin and his friend.

'I saw what you did,' said Gudrun, hurrying close. 'Is it still alive?'

'I don't know,' said Hal.

Gudrun took the puppy from Hal and wrapped it in the woollen folds of her tunic. She rubbed it and spoke to it and blew on its face.

'It moved! Keep doing that,' urged Hal.

The puppy opened its mouth and made a tiny sound.

'Let me have a go now,' said Hal. 'Please, Gudrun? It is my puppy.'

'It's a boy,' said Gudrun. 'What's his name?'

Hal thought of Grandfather, strong and kind and funny. 'I'll call him Olaf after Grandfather,' said Hal.

'Uncle Ivar isn't going to let you have him here,' said Gudrun. 'But my father might take him. Our dog is getting old.'

'But he's mine!' said Hal.

'Then how will you keep him?'

'I'll hide him,' he said.

Hal was shivering with cold now. A woman with a small child perched on her hip was calling to him from outside a longhouse below.

'It's my mother,' said Hal. 'I have to go.'

'Then leave Olaf with me. I'll care for him,' said Gudrun.

Hal handed the puppy over. 'I'll be back for him soon,' he said. He set off down the track.

CHAPTER 3

'HOWEVER DID YOU get
so wet?' asked Hal's mother
when she saw him. 'I've been
looking for you. I have news.'

'Boat!' said Alfrun, wriggling on
her mother's hip.

'Boat?' asked Hal. 'Am I to go fishing?'

'No,' said his mother. 'We are to leave.
Your uncle says that we must.'

'Leave here? Why? Where will
we go?'

Hal's mother put a hand
on his curly wet head.
'Hal, love, when your
father did not
come home, your
grandfather was
happy for us to go
on living with
him. But now that
Grandfather is dead,

Uncle Ivar, as his eldest son, inherits everything. Ivar wants to take a wife and have children of his own. He cannot support his dead brother's wife and children as well. We must go.'

'But where to?' asked Hal.

'To England. They need women and children to make homes for the men who are already there.

Think, Hal, we'll have a new life in a new land, away from the sadness of all that has happened here.'

Hal looked up at her.

'Do they need dogs in England?'

'Dogs?'

'Yes. Would it be good to have a faithful guard dog like Freya?'

Hal's mother looked up to Thor's Hammer and saw Gudrun holding something. 'Oh, Hal, now I understand. Freya's puppies?'

'Just one of them,' said Hal.

'Against your uncle's word? Perhaps it is as well that we are to leave! Come, let's get you dry,' said his mother. 'Then you had better hurry to your uncle's jobs and confess about that puppy. It will need some food.'

'Will we ever come back here?' asked Hal.

'No,' said his mother. She quickly turned away and headed towards the dairy with Alfrun running after her.

CHAPTER 4

AS HAL SAT by the fire that evening, he gazed at the carved posts that held up the great longhouse roof. They were carved up and down and around with creatures and patterns and gods from the great sagas that he had heard so often around evening fires. Hal loved them. When he was little, he had watched his father's knife stroking sweet-smelling shavings from the wood to find gods and winding snakes and dragon heads.

He had watched Father carving Ran, goddess of the sea. Now she had taken Father for her own, deep down below the sea.

The carving of Ran seemed to come alive now in the flickering firelight, frightening Hal with thoughts of the voyage that he must make across her sea.

Those carvings made Hal remember his father's frown as he worked. It was a frown that opened into a smile when he looked up and saw Hal watching. In a way, the carvings meant that Hal's dead father still had a kind of life in the homestead. But now Hal must leave them behind. He must go and live in another place.

Hal leant across to his mother and asked her, 'What is England like?'

Hal had heard stories of how
Grandfather, and his father before
him, had sailed to England and
Scotland and Ireland. They
had fought fiercely and
killed many and brought
home treasure
and slaves.

Old Cuthbert who worked with the homestead horses had been taken from England when he was Hal's age. Cuthbert was different from the rest of them. He believed in only one god. He spoke strangely, and seemed sad all the time. Was that what all the English people were like?

'Will the people fight us like they fought Grandfather?' asked Hal.

'No,' said his mother. 'Our people have been settled for so long now that we are no longer enemies. Cousin Inga is there. She is married to a native man and they tell me that she speaks the language and behaves more like one of them than one of us now.'

'Good,' whispered Hal. He knew it was shameful, but he did not want to use a sword on another person, at least not until he was

a fully-grown man. He asked his mother, 'Do
you think that I could carve roof posts for our
new home? Like Father did here?'

'You can try,' she replied. 'But carving is
a great skill and it takes patience.'

'I want to show the story of our crossing
to the new country,' said Hal. 'And later I
will make posts for the old sagas too.'

Hal pulled a log from the pile of firewood to
practice on. He took the knife that he kept in
his waist pouch and he began to whittle away
the bark to the bright white wood underneath.
He worked a head with a nose and ears and
rubbed it smooth with a thumb and held it to
the firelight. It didn't look very much like Olaf,
but you could tell that it was a dog.
My post will show Olaf's saga,
decided Hal. Olaf, born from
his mother, then born
again from the sea,
and kept alive so that
he can protect us in
the new country.

CHAPTER 5

OVER THE WEEKS of summer, Hal was kept busy preparing for the voyage. Over those same weeks, Olaf grew from a dumpy, fluffy puppy to a lanky young dog. Whenever he could, Hal and Gudrun would take Olaf to the fields to train him.

'I want him to be as obedient as Freya was,' said Hal. 'He'll be our guard dog in England and he'll help us catch food.'

'I have heard that over there they make great
buildings in honour of their god,' said Gudrun.
'They say that it is a warmer place and not so
dark in the winter as it is here. And land lies
flat for sheep and cows as far as you can see.'
Gudrun clutched her hands together. 'Oh, I
wish that I could come with you, Hal. I'll be
stuck in this same place for my whole life. You
are lucky!'

'But I'll never see this homestead or our fjord
again,' said Hal.

'Will you forget it?'

'No,' said Hal. 'I am making a roof post from one of our trees that will tell the story of it all. Uncle Ivar cut me the post and I have already begun carving Grandfather with his great sword, and Olaf being born.'

Gudrun flicked her long plait over her shoulder. 'Am I in the story?' she asked. 'Am I on the post?'

'There isn't room for everything,' said Hal. 'I'm going to start on the ship soon.'

CHAPTER 6

THEY CLIMBED UP to Thor's Hammer to see the ship arrive.

'Where is it?' asked little Alfrun.

'It will come on the tide,' Hal told her.

'Come now!' said Alfrun. She and Olaf raced around in circles. Gudrun smiled at Hal, 'She doesn't understand, does she?'

'Not really,' agreed Hal, and he almost wished that he didn't understand what a very big thing was about to happen to them.

The dumpy trading ship came around the bend in the fjord and sailed towards them over gleaming water. Distant sailors, tiny as ants, pulled down the great square sail and stuck oars out either side to row the ship ashore.

The oars made the boat look like Odin's eight-
legged horse, thought Hal. That must be
a good omen. Hal suddenly smiled, excited
like Alfrun after all.

'Come on!' He grabbed Alfrun's hand and
began to hurry her down the steep slope.

They loaded the ship with sheep, a goat and
chickens that Uncle Ivar had given them for
their new home. And there were barrels of
water and beer, and tubs of barley and
honey and dried peas. Mother's precious
amber necklace, and the drinking horn
rimmed with silver that Father had brought
from the east, were tied in a leather bag.

Furs and blankets were bundled and bound.
Tools and Hal's roof post were all carefully
stowed aboard.

Hal's mother settled with Alfrun on a pile
of furs.

'Time you went aboard too, Hal,' said Uncle
Ivar. Hal glanced at Gudrun. She was crying.
Hal looked away. He bent and picked up
a pebble. Then he called Olaf and together
they stepped up the plank and into the ship.
It swayed gently in the lapping water.

There were shouts and pushing and suddenly
Hal was adrift from the land that had always
been his home. The sailors shouted orders
and tugged on ropes to raise the sail flapping
and filling with wind. As the ship sailed
away down the fjord, Hal watched his home
shrinking. The captain of the ship called over
to Hal.

'Come up here, lad, if you want a good view.'

So Hal clambered over to join the captain
on the afterdeck, where he stood with one
hand on the tiller of the steering oar. Behind
were the steep sides of the fjord. Ahead lay
the endless, empty glittering sea.

'How far to England?' asked Hal.

'A good three days travel,' said the captain.
'Somewhere over that horizon.'

Hal breathed in the salty, windy air and closed
his eyes and prayed that they would all get
there safely.

CHAPTER 7

DARKNESS CAME AND people and animals slept, but the sea didn't sleep and neither did Hal. The lurching boat made him feel ill. He held warm Olaf and stroked the dog's soft ears.

The storm came on dark clouds, whistling through the rigging and slapping angry great waves against the wooden sides of the ship and spitting spray in Hal's face. Hal took the pebble from his pouch and turned it over and over in his fingers. The pebble was the only bit of land he had now.

Dawn lightened the sky a little, but the wind blew stronger and the boat heaved and creaked. The sailors pulled down the great wet sail and tried to steer the ship into the waves. Cold hard rain blew at them. Hal's mother put one arm around Alfrun and one around Hal.

But a sudden shout from the captain made them all look up to see a great wave gathering itself up and up, and then down it came to try to drown them all.

'No!' shrieked Hal's mother and she grabbed for her daughter, but the water snatched Alfrun and threw her into the sea. 'NO!'

'Alfrun!' shouted Hal. He reached out to grab Alfrun's red cloak while his mother tried desperately to hold onto him, to keep him safe with her. But the ship tipped and Hal slipped. Suddenly he was alone in cold water that rolled him and roared and gagged his mouth when he gasped. Hal thrashed his arms and legs and didn't know which way was up or down.

Then he saw something red and he took hold
of it and pulled the solid little body of Alfrun
to him, but he needed air or they would both
be trapped with goddess Ran forever. Suddenly
Hal heard a sharp yapping sound and knew
that Olaf was calling to him from the
boat. He kicked and saw light and
came bursting into air for just long
enough to gasp a breath before
water slapped in his face again.

There were shouts, and Alfrun was lifted from Hal's arms. He could swim again now, but the side of the ship was like a great moving wall in front of him, and he had no strength left and no way to climb it. He knew that those who fell overboard were nearly always lost. Hal was sinking into numb exhaustion when the sound of Olaf's sharp yap deepening into a proper bark came into his brain. Then something hard hit Hal on the shoulder and he reached out and took firm hold of something wooden. He was lifted from the sea.

Hal lay within the ship and coughed up
seawater. He shook with shock and cold.
Olaf's hot tongue licked his face as they
wrapped him in a fur and rubbed his feet.

'Alfrun?' asked Hal.

'Safe beside you,' his mother told him as she
stroked wet hair from his eyes. 'You saved her,
Hal. You are both safe. Ran has been good
to us.'

They sacrificed the goat and gave it to Ran
in thanks for the lives spared. And the goddess
was pleased. The sky lightened and the wind
blew less wildly. The sailors raised the great
sail again.

Hal told Olaf, 'I heard you barking. You
helped to save me. Grandfather would be
proud of you. So would Gudrun. I'll carve it all
on the roof post.'

'It was your roof post that the sailors used to

fish you from the sea,' Hal's mother told
him. Hal looked at the carved post and saw
something new.

'What's that there?' he asked. 'I didn't carve
that!' He pointed to a small figure that had been
cut into the wood. The figure had a triangle of
tunic with feet below it. 'It's a girl,' said Hal.

The girl had a criss-cross line running from
her head down her left shoulder. 'It's Gudrun!'
Hal scowled. 'She's spoiled it!'

'No, she hasn't,' said his mother. 'She just
wanted to be part of your saga.'

'She did say that she wanted to come too.'
Hal touched the little figure
of Gudrun. 'Maybe she
really will come
one day.'

'Maybe,' said
his mother.

CHAPTER 8

THE MEMORY OF nearly drowning stayed with Hal and he used that memory to carve the story on his roof post over the next two days.

Then, at last, land was sighted. Olaf lifted his head and seemed to sniff and hear something new in the air, and his stumpy tail wagged. As they got closer, the land grew to fill the whole of the horizon. It was a strange land, flat and green. Hal told Alfrun, 'That's our new home.' He squeezed her small grubby hand tight.

It felt to Hal, at first, as if the new land wasn't a solid kind of land at all.

When he waded through the shallow sea onto the beach, the land seemed to sway under him. The sailors laughed. 'Don't worry,' they told him. 'You'll soon get your land legs back.'

There were people on the beach, watching
as the animals and goods were brought off
the ship. They spoke and laughed words that
Hal didn't understand and they were dressed
strangely. But it is me who is the stranger,
thought Hal with a shock. He suddenly felt lost.

But Olaf ran joyfully towards a group of boys
who had a big dog with them. Olaf crouched
low and let the big dog sniff him. Both their
tails wagged. In moments, they were bounding

off over the beach together. Is making new
friends really that easy? wondered Hal.
He looked at the boys. Two of them seemed
wary, but the younger one grinned back.

'Hal!' called his mother. 'Come and meet
Cousin Inga. She's come to meet us and take
us to her home. Her sons will help carry our
things. That great roof post of yours will be
a test of strength, but four boys should
manage it.'

So the boys were from Hal's own family!
Hal reached into his pouch for the pebble that
he had carried from home. He threw it into
the mass of pebbles on this beach. The pebble
from home was instantly lost in the mass of
rounded stones, all similar but each of them
different.

The youngest boy cousin beckoned with his
hand. You didn't always need words in order
to understand what somebody means.

'I'm coming!' smiled Hal, and he ran to join them in lifting his roof post and carrying it up onto the new land.

THE VIKINGS

Hi. My name is Hal, and I am a Viking. Let me tell you more about my people.

My people, the Vikings, came from the Scandinavian countries; Denmark, Sweden and Norway. In Britain, they called us Norse people because we came from the North.

The Vikings were mostly farmers, but some worked as craftsmen or traders. But they were also brilliant inventors, great travellers and skilled ship builders. They sailed far and wide in their wooden longships which were strong and lightweight.

They didn't have any navigational tools, but they managed to find their way over long distances using the sun, the stars and the direction of the wind.

Some of my people were fierce warriors. They raided other countries for treasures and slaves. In 789 AD, the Vikings raided Britain for the first time.

These Viking raiders often attacked important Christian sites, like monasteries and churches. The British thought they were trying to destroy Christianity, but the warriors were more interested in

the treasures they found inside. The British Christians had only one god. When my people first arrived in Britain, they followed their own religion and worshipped lots of different gods.

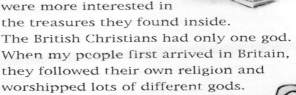

The stories about our gods are known as Norse Myths. Here are three of our gods.

Odin was the god of magic, poetry and war.

Thor ruled the skies, thunder and storms.

Freyr was the goddess of love and fertility.

Most of my people who sailed overseas were simply searching for better land for their farms. Gradually, the violent raids gave way to a period of settlement. My own family made their home in Britain and lived peacefully with the inhabitants, farming as we had done at home.

This is the inside of my new house. We lived a very different life from people today. Can you spot all the differences?

For a long time, much of what was known about the Vikings came from the people who had been attacked by them, such as monks.

Nowadays, thanks to archaeology, there is a clearer picture of where my people lived in Britain and how they influenced British life. If you go to your local museum, you might see Viking artefacts that have been discovered in your area.

Look! This post tells a story.

CAN YOU WRITE LIKE A VIKING?

The Vikings had their own alphabet made up of special letters called runes. Each rune had a particular sound, but it also had a special meaning of its own.

To the Vikings the runes had magical powers. Experts called Rune Masters were called on to cast spells by carving particular runes.

THIS IS THE RUNIC ALPHABET OR 'FUTHARK'.

a b c d e f g h ij k l

m n o p q r s t uvw x y z

What message has Hal written at the bottom of his post?

Why don't you try writing your name in runes?